1 Silly Cow
in the Schoharie Valley
A POLLY HOLLER GANG COUNTING BOOK

To Aven!

Be Silly! LiN

Count on!, Deb

Copyright © 2017 by Lin Quinn

Published by Under the Nose, LLC
207 Mill Valley Road | Middleburgh NY 12122 | UnderTheNose.com/Books

D1279395

1 silly cow pauses, almost hiding while seeking.

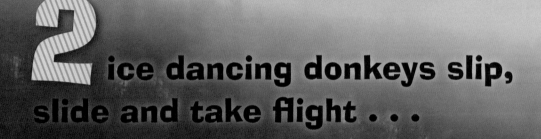 **2 ice dancing donkeys slip, slide and take flight . . .**

and 1 silly cow.

3 fancy goats dab, dob and splash . . .

and **1** silly cow.

4 dapper pigs wait for the birthday bash to begin . . .

and 1 silly cow.

6 spry hounds pitter pat on the fall fruit . . .

and **1** silly cow.

8 decked out ducks enjoy a snowy hullabaloo . . .

and 1 silly cow.

9 wind blown chicks in awe of the great Yogini . . .

and **1** silly cow.

10 fun-loving friends pause before their new adventure . . .

LEARN MORE. . .

Vroman's Nose, a popular hiking trail, is located ½ a mile outside the quaint Village of Middleburgh, NY. The trailhead is located in Polly Holler, a small neighborhood on Mill Valley Road and is one of the original settlements in Schoharie County.

HERE'S SOME INFORMATION ABOUT THE PHOTOS

Cover – Vroman's Nose, as seen from Middleburgh

1 cow – Vroman's Nose Hiking Trail, Town of Fulton

2 donkeys – Schoharie County Pond

3 goats – #18 Autumn Splendor, Schoharie County Quilt Barn Trail

4 pigs – Fox Creek Covered Bridge, Schoharie

5 sheep – Schoharie County

6 hounds – Barber's Farm Pumpkin Field with view of Vroman's Nose

7 cats – Schoharie Creek

8 ducks – Schoharie County

9 chicks – Top of Vroman's Nose, view of the Schoharie Valley

10 friends – Schoharie County

ABOUT THE AUTHOR / ILLUSTRATOR & PHOTOGRAPHER

Lin Quinn, Author / Illustrator

Lin, "the happy cow lady", is a published author, illustrator, graphic artist, potter, wife, mother/mother-in-law to six adult children and a Nana/Gammy to her beautiful grand babies. Lin began drawing and writing at a very young age and has spent a lifetime exploring and teaching her craft with others. Her work is featured at her gift shop, Under The Nose, located at the trailhead of Vroman's Nose where she and her husband cater to the many travellers looking for snacks and mementos upon completing their hike.

LinQuinn.com | Facebook.com/LinQuinnAuthorIllustrator | UnderTheNose.com/Books

Debra Bechtold, Photographer

Debra is a talented photographer, watercolor artist, sculpturalist, gardener, wife and mother of two young men. Debra has photographed Vroman's Nose and the surrounding area since relocating to Middleburgh in 1988. Debra's photos can be seen on her Visions of Schoharie Valley Facebook page, in a travelling exhibit created for the Schoharie County Quilt Barn Trail, in local businesses and featured at Under the Nose.

Facebook.com/visionsofschoharievalley | Facebook.com/Debra Bechtold_Graphic Artist

MORE ABOUT THE AREA

Schoharie County - VisitSchoharieCounty.com
Schoharie Valley - SchoharieValley.org
Middleburgh, NY - MiddleburghNY.com

This book and other Polly Holler Gang products are available for purchase at

Under the Nose Gift & Goodie Shop

207 Mill Valley Road, Middleburgh NY, 12122 | UnderTheNose.com

**To Find Other
POLLY HOLLER GANG BOOKS
visit**

LinQuinn.com
Facebook.com/LinQuinnAuthorIllustrator
UnderTheNose.com/Books

This book is dedicated to my amazing husband,
our three children, their partners and especially
my grand babies . . .

without each and every one of you,
this would not have happened!

THANK YOU!

Made in the USA
Columbia, SC
25 September 2017